THE WIND IN THE WILLOWS

Abridged by John Broadhead
Illustrated by Kate Simpson

CARNIVAL

THE RIVER BANK

After a long winter sleep in his little house under the ground, Mole wanted to see the world again.

He climbed up through the earth and found himself in a big field. The sun was shining brightly.

"How lovely!" he cried. "Spring is here again!"

He walked happily through many meadows and came to a great river. On the other side a little brown creature with bright eyes and thick silky hair was coming out of a dark hole just above the water. It was Water Rat.

"Hullo!" shouted Rat, stepping into a little blue boat. "Do you want me to bring you across?"

He rowed over and helped Mole into the boat.

"This is wonderful!" said Mole, who had never been in a boat before.

"I'm pleased that you like it," smiled Rat. He pointed to a basket filled with tasty sandwiches. "If you have time, you can come on a picnic with me."

"Yes, please!" cried Mole, sitting back.

"I *love* the river," said Rat, rowing strongly. "I wouldn't live anywhere else."

"What's over there?" asked Mole, pointing to a large, dark wood.

"Oh, that's the Wild Wood. We small animals never go there. It can be dangerous," said Rat rather sadly. "Dear old Badger lives in the middle of it!"

Soon they came to a little lake. Rat tied up the boat, and they sat on the bank and ate their sandwiches.

"It's busy on the river today," smiled Rat, watching Toad row past, making a loud splashing noise as he did so. "He'll fall in if he isn't careful!"

On the way home, Mole suddenly stood up in the boat and took the oars from Rat. "Let *me* row!"

"Look out!" cried Rat, but it was too late. The boat wobbled and turned over, throwing the two of them into the river.

Rat caught Mole and brought him safely to the bank. Then he swam back to fetch the boat and the picnic basket.

"I'm so sorry," said Mole, miserable and wet.

"Don't worry!" answered Rat gently. "Come and stay at my house. I'll teach you to row and swim."

So back they went to Rat's cosy little home, where they lit a fire and had some tea. Rat sat with Mole and told him funny stories about the river and the animals who lived there.

Soon they were feeling sleepy and Rat showed Mole to his room.

As soon as his head touched the pillow, Mole fell fast asleep and dreamed of his first day by the river.

"Ratty," said Mole one bright morning. "Can we call and see Toad?"

"What a good idea!" answered Rat. "We'll go at once!"

They jumped into the little blue boat and paddled off down the river until they reached a huge old house with a long garden.

"This is Toad Hall," said Rat, as they walked across the grass.

Toad jumped up from his armchair in delight when he saw his visitors. "Hooray! It's lucky you've come today!"

"Why?" asked Rat. "Do you want me to show you how to row properly?"

"Poo, no more boats for *me*!" whooped Toad. "I've found something much better. Come and see!"

He led them to a beautiful gypsy caravan, complete with cooker, pots, pans, jugs and kettles.

"Hop in," said Toad, taking the reins of his old grey horse. "We're going to travel the countryside."

"But we can't –" began Mole.

"Nonsense!" cried Toad. "You must come!"

And go they did! They spent the day travelling along narrow lanes, up and down hills and through little villages. The sun shone, birds whistled to them, and rabbits waved as they drove slowly on.

Suddenly they heard a loud noise from behind.

"Poop-poop! Poop-poop!" A big car with an open top raced past them with a great roar. The old grey horse was scared and ran into a ditch. With a mighty crash the caravan fell onto its side.

"Road hog!" yelled Rat in anger, shaking his fist at the car, which was now a long way off.

Mole thought Toad would be annoyed too, but he was not. He simply kept on saying to himself, "Poop-poop, poop-poop!"

"Will you help fix the caravan, Toad?" asked Rat.

"Poo, no more caravans for *me*!" said Toad. "Forget caravans. It's a motor-car for me from now on. There simply is no better way to travel!"

Rat sighed, and then, with Mole and the old grey horse, set off walking the long journey home, listening to Toad talking excitedly about the motor-car he was going to buy!

THE WILD WOOD

Summer came to an end at last, and Mole had had many exciting adventures – but he had still not met Badger.

So one cold afternoon, when Rat was sleeping by the fireside, he set off for the Wild Wood.

"It can't be *too* bad," he thought.

Everything was very still and it was getting dark. Poor Mole started to glance behind; he felt as if someone was following him.

Then the faces began! Everywhere he looked he thought he saw evil little eyes peeping at him.

He heard a low whistling noise and then the sound of pattering feet. In panic he began to run, falling over and going round and round in circles.

Finally, he plunged into the hollow of an old beech tree and snuggled up in some dry leaves. He lay there, panting and listening to the strange noises.

Back home, Rat awoke and found that Mole was not there. When he saw that Mole's cap and shoes were missing from the peg, he went outside.

"Oh, no!" he cried, seeing Mole's footprints in the mud leading to the Wild Wood. He took up a stick and ran after him.

Rat hated being in the wood, but he simply had to find his friend.

"Mole! Mole!" he shouted, as he walked around.

After an hour he heard a little voice cry, "Ratty! Is that really you?"

Rat crept into the hollow and found Mole, who was very pleased to see him. They had a short rest and then decided to return home.

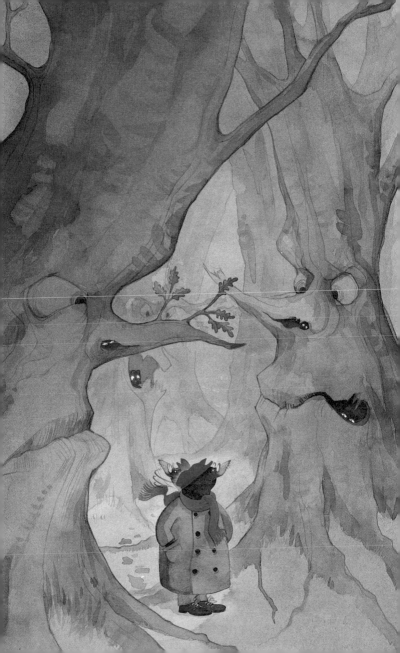

It was very dark now and it was snowing too.

"Are we lost?" asked Mole after an hour or two.

Rat was about to say that they were indeed lost,
when he noticed a small green door on the side of a
mound of earth. He ran to it, pulling Mole with him.

"Look!" He pointed to a neat sign which said, 'Mr
Badger'. "We're safe now! Ring the bell . . ."

The door opened and there stood Badger.

"Ratty! Do come in – both of you!" he said.

Rat and Mole followed Badger down a long tunnel
into a large kitchen where there was a fire. Badger
gave each of them a warm, dry dressing-gown and
invited them to the table for a meal.

"How is Toad these days?" asked Badger. "Did he
ever buy a motor-car?"

"I'll say he did!" laughed Rat. "He's a terrible
driver."

"He's had seven crashes already!" added Mole.

"Oh, dear!" said Badger thoughtfully. "As his
friends, we really should do something to help him."

Rat and Mole finished their meal and spent a
happy evening in the company of Badger.

They stayed the night, and next morning had
breakfast with Badger and two young hedgehogs and
Otter, who had called to see him.

"See you again soon, Badger, and thank you for
making us so welcome," smiled Rat, as he and Mole
prepared to leave. "I'll take you both to the edge of the
Wood," said Otter. "You'll be quite safe with me!"

Otter said goodbye and left them at the edge of the
Wild Wood. They turned and took a last look at the
grim forest, with its tall trees poking their way
through the blanket of snow on the ground.

BACK HOME

The two animals plodded on through the snow.
They felt cold and tired. It was hard to walk, and
Mole was going slower and slower.

"Come along, Mole," said Rat cheerfully.

"Oh, *please* let us stop for a moment!" pleaded
Mole. "I used to live round here."

He sniffed at the ground, then suddenly dived into
the deep snow. Rat followed and found him standing
at a tiny front door.

Mole's house, once so tidy, was now very dusty.

"Oh, Ratty, why did I bring you to this poor, cold
little place?" he sighed.

"Nonsense!" said Rat, lighting some candles. "It's
beautiful. Fetch a duster, while I light the fire."

Soon Mole's house was warm and cosy. Rat was sitting at the table and opening a tin of fish. He heard tiny voices outside. "What's that?" he asked.

Mole opened the door. There in the light of a lantern stood eight field-mice wearing red scarves.

A shrill chorus of high voices then sang a lovely Christmas carol. Mole and Rat listened in delight.

Mole invited the singers inside. There they spent a pleasant evening together, sharing Mole's food.

By the time their guests had left, Mole and Rat were very sleepy. Mole showed Rat to the spare bed and then tumbled into bed.

"I love my new life by the river," he said to himself as he lay on his tiny pillow, "but it's good to have a place of my own to come back to whenever I want!"

He closed his eyes and fell asleep.

TOAD'S ADVENTURES

It was now early summer. Mole and Rat were sitting in Rat's living-room, making plans.

A knock came at the door. It was Badger.

"Hullo, Badger," said Rat. "How nice to see you!"

"The time has come for us to call on Toad!" murmured Badger gravely. "He has ordered a big new motor-car. We must stop him from driving before he hurts himself!"

The three animals hurried round to Toad Hall immediately. There they found Toad sitting in a huge red motor-car. Dressed in a new coat, hat and goggles.

"Just in time to come for a ride with me!" he said.

"Sorry, that's just where you're wrong!" cried Badger. "*You're* going to your room, Toad."

Badger, Rat and Mole took hold of Toad and laid him, kicking and shouting, on the floor. They pulled off his silly coat, hat and goggles and marched him firmly up the long stairs of Toad Hall. They led him to his bedroom, pushed him in and locked the door.

"It's for your own good, Toady!" shouted Badger through the keyhole. "We don't want you to have another crash!"

"Oh, bother!" said Toad angrily.

The three friends took it in turn to go into Toad's room and keep him company. But next morning, when Rat was with him, Toad put his hands on his tummy and groaned.

"What's wrong?" asked Rat in alarm.

"I need a doctor," moaned Toad.

"Oh, dear! Don't worry, Toad – I'll get some help!" cried Rat, and he ran off to the village.

It was a trick, of course! As soon as Rat had disappeared, Toad laughed out loud. "Poor old Ratty. He'll be in trouble when Badger and Mole return!"

He put on his best suit, filled his pockets with lots of money and left Toad Hall. He walked for miles until he came to a small town.

As he passed a hotel, he heard a noise that he knew very well, it was the sound of a car horn!

"Poop, poop!" went the horn, as the car stopped outside the hotel. The driver and his passengers went inside, leaving the motor-car quite alone.

"I wonder if it *starts* easily?" thought Toad, walking slowly around it.

In a moment he had jumped into the driver's seat and was roaring away down the street! Faster and faster he went, out of the town and through the open countryside.

"This is the life for me!" he grinned, as the wind blew hard in his face.

He held the steering-wheel tightly and pressed hard on the pedal with his foot. . .

The next morning Toad opened his eyes and looked around. Where was he? Not in his warm bed at Toad Hall, but in a dark, cold prison cell!

Now he remembered what had happened the day before. How he had taken the motor-car, how he had been chased by policemen and been taken to court. Then that nasty judge had told him he would be in jail for twenty years.

"Twenty years!" said Toad sadly, holding his head in his hands. "If only I'd listened to Ratty, Mole and Badger!"

Over the next few days the jailer's daughter brought him his meals. She felt sorry for him and became his friend.

"Would you like to get out of here?" she said one afternoon.

"More than anything in the world!" he answered.

"Good. I have a plan," she said. "My aunt will be coming to take away your dirty washing tomorrow night. When she comes, you can change into her clothes and just walk out!"

And that is exactly what Toad did!

"I must look awfully odd," he laughed, as he walked to the railway station, "but at least I'm *free!*"

Silly Toad had left all his money in jail and could not buy a train ticket to take him back to Toad Hall. He started to cry.

"Hullo, old lady," said the cheerful engine-driver. "What's the matter?"

Toad told him that he had no money and that he was miles from home.

"Poor thing!" said the driver, still thinking that Toad was an old washerwoman. "You can ride home with me in the engine!"

Toad was filled with joy and he jumped on board. The train moved off into the dark night.

They chugged along for miles. Toad was very hungry and wondered what to have for supper. Then, noticing that the engine-driver was staring behind, he sat up and took a look too. Another train was following them!

"It's full of policemen and prison warders!" said the engine-driver. "They're all shouting, 'Stop!'"

"Oh, don't stop, please!" cried Toad, falling to his knees. "I'm not really a washerwoman! I'm Mr Toad and I've escaped from a horrid dungeon. Don't let them take me back!"

The engine driver looked down sternly at him and asked, "Why were you in prison?"

"I borrowed a motor-car. I didn't mean to *steal* it!"

"I hate to see an animal in tears, Mr Toad," said the engine-driver. "I'll help you!"

The train roared into a long, black tunnel. As soon as they came out of it, the driver put on his brakes and stopped the train. Toad jumped out, rolled down a short slope and ran into a wood.

Peeping out, he saw his train start up again and disappear at great speed. Out of the tunnel came the second engine, still chasing the first. Toad had a good laugh at this clever trick!

But he soon stopped laughing when he realised that he was alone in this strange wood so far from home.

Hungry and tired, he found a hollow tree filled with dead leaves. It made a comfortable bed, so Toad lay down and slept soundly.

Toad wouldn't have slept at all if he had known what was happening back at Toad Hall.

The Stoats and Weasels – most unfriendly creatures from the Wild Wood – had found the place empty and had quickly moved into it! Mole, Badger, Ratty and the other animals from the river-bank had tried to stop them, but had not been able to do so.

So now Toad's grand home was overrun with these unwelcome guests, who lay in bed half the day, ate his food, drank his tea and coffee, and made up jokes and horrible songs about him.

MORE ADVENTURES

The warm sunshine woke Toad early next morning. He brushed himself down and set off through the wood.

He saw a road and walked along it in the hope that it might take him home; and he sang a little song to cheer himself up.

Then came a sound that he knew well. It was the poop-poop of a horn! In the distance was a motor-car.

"Maybe they'll give me a lift!" he said excitedly, waving at the car.

But his face went suddenly pale and his knees turned to jelly. It was the car he had taken from outside the hotel! He fell to the ground crying, "Oh, no! They'll take me back to prison!"

The car stopped and two men got out. They walked across to Toad and picked him up.

"This poor washerwoman has fainted," said one. "Let's take her to the nearest village."

They placed Toad carefully on the back seat and made him comfortable. He opened one eye.

"She looks better already!" whispered one of the men kindly.

"Thank you, sir, I feel better," murmured Toad feebly. "May I sit at the front and get more fresh air?"

"Of course!" said one of the men, helping Toad into the front seat.

As they purred along, Toad couldn't wait to get his hands on the steering-wheel. He asked politely if he could drive.

"Yes, alright!" said the driver, stopping the car and moving out of his seat. "Please *do*!"

At first Toad drove gently along the road, but one of the men shouted, "Please be careful, washerwoman!" as they started to go too quickly.

Toad was no longer listening. He went even faster and cried, "Ho, ho! I'm Toad, the motor-car thief! *I'll* show you how to drive properly!"

By now he was going far too fast. He crashed through a hedge and drove into a fishpond. He flew through the air and landed with a bump in a soft green meadow, picked himself up and scrambled away as quickly as he could.

When he thought he was safe, he slowed down and began to sing again – about how clever he was! But not for long, because he saw two policemen running towards him. In his panic, he didn't see the river that lay ahead. He fell into it and was carried away by the strong flow of water.

He floated along helplessly, trying in vain to grab hold of reeds. Finally, he saw a dark hole in the bank and stretched out an arm to catch hold of the edge of it. With a huge effort he pulled himself out of the water and into the hole.

Out of the blackness appeared a pair of twinkling eyes; and then a face – brown and small, with whiskers, neat ears and silky hair.

It was Water Rat!

RETURN TO TOAD HALL

"**Y**ou mean to *say*," yelled Toad, waving his arms in alarm, "that those wretched Wild Wooders have taken over my beautiful Hall? I'll go at once."

He was resting with his feet up on the comfortable couch in Rat's front room. Mole and Badger were there too.

" Calm down, Toad. You can't do anything alone. They have guards at the gate," said Badger softly.

"The *cheek* of it!" shouted Toad.

"Can't we help him?" asked Mole.

"Yes, we can!" smiled Badger. "You see, I know of a secret underground passage leading from the River bank right into the middle of Toad Hall!"

"Nonsense!" snapped Toad. "There *isn't* one!"

"Yes, there is," said Badger firmly. "Your father told me about it many years ago – and tonight we're going to use it!"

When it began to grow dark, Badger, Mole, Rat and Toad walked silently along the edge of the river. Each of them wore a stick in a belt – just like a sword – and Badger also carried a tiny lantern.

"This is the entrance," whispered Badger, pointing to a small hole in the River bank. "Follow me!"

The four adventurers crept along the dark, damp passage. Toad shivered in fear but he tried to be brave.

"We must be under the Hall now," said Badger as the passage started to slope upwards.

From above came the sound of animals enjoying themselves: singing, tapping their little feet and clinking glasses.

"They're having a *party*!" snorted Toad.

The four hurried along to the end of the passage and found themselves below a wooden trapdoor.

"Altogether now – *push*!" cried Badger.

The trapdoor opened and they climbed up to the kitchen of Toad Hall. They took out their sticks and waited for the command from Badger.

"*Now*!" he yelled and flung open the big doors to the dining-hall.

What a squealing and screeching filled the air!

Terrified weasels and stoats dived under the tables, ran up the chimney and jumped through open windows. Badger, Mole and Rat ran about, whirling their sticks in the air and whooping loudly. Toad chased the Chief Weasel over the table full of food and out through the door. To the scared weasels and stoats the room seemed to be filled with monstrous animals, grey, black, brown and green .

Soon it was over and the unwanted animals had fled in terror. Toad Hall belonged to Toad once more!

The mess was cleared up and there was another party very shortly afterwards. But this time there were no weasels or stoats: just Toad, Mole, Rat, Badger and all their friends from the river-bank.

Toad was a different fellow after his adventures, and promised never to drive a motor-car again! He bought a beautiful gold chain and locket, which he sent to the jailer's daughter. Then he found the engine-driver who had helped him, and gave him a handsome reward.

The four friends continued to live their lives in great joy and contentment. On long summer evenings they would often walk through the Wild Wood, as they now had no fear of the animals who lived there.

Sometimes mother weasels would point at them and say, "Look, baby! There go the great Mr Toad, brave Water Rat and the famous Mr Mole!" And when the children were naughty they would be told that the terrible grey Badger would come and get them.

It wasn't true of course, because we all know that Badger was really rather fond of children!

First published in this abridged version by Carnival in 1988.

Carnival is an imprint of
the Children's Division, part of
the Collins Publishing Group,
8 Grafton Street, London W1X 3LA

Illustrations © Kate Simpson, 1988

Printed and bound in Great Britain by
PURNELL BOOK PRODUCTION LIMITED
A Member of BPCC plc